Colin McNaughton

GUESS WHO'S JUST MOVED IN NEXT DOOR?

Random House 🏠 New York

For May and Tom!

Library of Congress Cataloging-in-Publication Data
McNaughton, Colin.
Guess who's just moved in next door/Colin McNaughton
p. cm.
Summary: A tour through a very peculiar neighborhood
where an assortment of wacky neighbors from Superman
to a ship of pirates reacts to the arrival of their new neighbors,
a normal human family.
ISBN 0-679-81802-2 (trade)
[1. Moving, Household—Fiction. 2. Neighborhood—Fiction.
3. Humorous stories. 4. Stories in rhyme.] I. Title.
PZ8.3.M46Hav 1991
[E]—dc20   90-46884

Manufactured in Hong Kong
10 9 8 7 6 5 4 3 2 1

We've a lovely bunch of people on our street;
    Yes, a nicer crowd you couldn't wish to meet.
But there's been an awful change –
    We've new neighbors; man, they're strange!
Can you guess who's just moved in
        Next door to us?

Let me introduce my friends; you will agree –
    Perfect neighbors, every one, as you will see.
But they'll be as shocked as me,
    As I'm certain you will be,
When they see who's just moved in
        Next door to us.

Say hello to Mister Thing;
    Squirting, squelching, slithering.
(Has he seen who's just moved in
    Next door to us?)

Meet the Dumptys – one's in bed;
    Took a tumble, cracked his head!
(Have they seen who's just moved in
    Next door to us?)

I'm afraid they get no thinner –
    They've a dozen eggs for dinner!
(Have they seen who's just moved in
    Next door to us?)

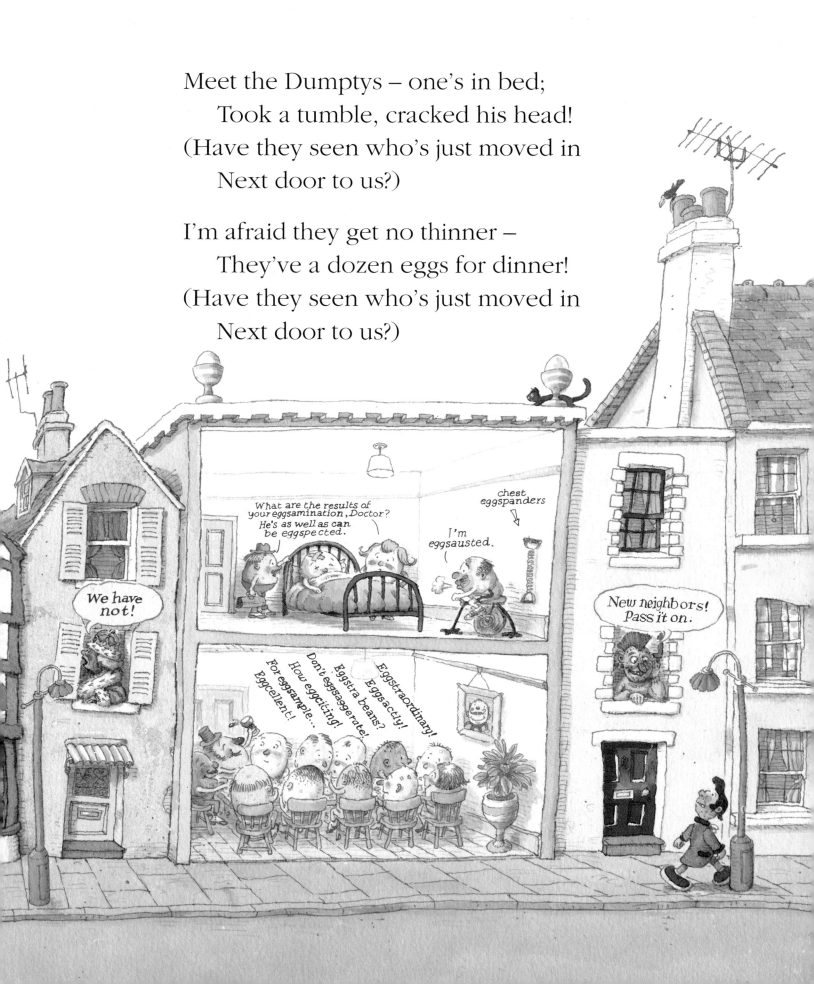

See the shop, it's just for pigs;
It sells plain and fancy wigs.
(Have they seen who's just moved in
Next door to us?)

And a school, it teaches birds
To say rude and silly words.
(Have they seen who's just moved in
Next door to us?)

Up in number twenty-four
Burglar Tom's got loot galore.
(Has he seen who's just moved in
Next door to us?)

Under Tom (I swear it's true!)
Are the local boys in blue.
(Have they seen who's just moved in
Next door to us?)

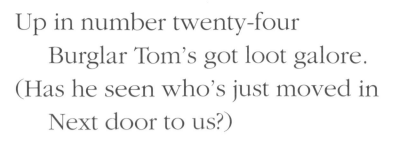

And further down the road,
  Salute the Duke of York's abode.
  (Has he seen who's just moved in
  Next door to us?)

An old lady with a broom,
  At number forty rents a room.
(Has she seen who's just moved in
  Next door to us?)

And living down below,
  We have Michelangelo.
(Has he seen who's just moved in
  Next door to us?)

Move five doors along:
   Say hello to Mister Kong.
(Has he seen who's just moved in
   Next door to us?)

Round the fountain in the park
    Swims a hammer-headed shark!
(Has it seen who's just moved in
    Next door to us?)

And piranhas, there's a school
    Cruising round the paddling pool.
(Have they seen who's just moved in
    Next door to us?)

See the creature, soft and rubbery,
  Hiding deep within the shrubbery.
(Has it seen who's just moved in
  Next door to us?)

And though the postman may complain,
  Here's where Tarzan lives with Jane.
(Have they seen who's just moved in
  Next door to us?)

Leather, denim, oil and grime –
 We've Hell's Angels (fifty-nine).
(Have they seen who's just moved in
 Next door to us?)

There's Mr. Thread (it's true, I swear),
 When he's in, he isn't there!
(Has he seen who's just moved in
 Next door to us?)

And at number seven-zero,
Meet a certain superhero.
(Has he seen who's just moved in
Next door to us?)

Though I know I shouldn't boast,
This house is haunted by a ghost.
(Has she seen who's just moved in
Next door to us?)

In the steeple lives a man,
   He keeps the belfry spick-and-span.
(Has he seen who's just moved in
   Next door to us?)

I've a hunch I know him well,
   It's his face that rings a bell.
(Has he seen who's just moved in
   Next door to us?)

In the graveyard by the church,
 Ghouls and ghosties limp and lurch.
(Have they seen who's just moved in
 Next door to us?)

At eighty-three the window lace
    Hides the folks from outer space.
(Have they seen who's just moved in
    Next door to us?)

And at number eighty-nine
    Lives my old friend Frankenstein.
(Has he seen who's just moved in
    Next door to us?)

Avast there, ninety-four!
  Abdul's pirates are ashore!
(Have they seen who's just moved in
  Next door to us?)

At one hundred an old fella,
  With horns, lives in the cellar.
(Has he seen who's just moved in
  Next door to us?)

There's a man above the dairy;
     When the moon shines, he gets hairy!
(Has he seen who's just moved in
     Next door to us?)

There is a sign at one-five-four;
    It reads "Danger – Dinosaur!"
(Has it seen who's just moved in
    Next door to us?)

Well, I hope you're feeling strong,
 Because now it won't be long
Till you see who's just moved in
 Next door to us.

Yes, the time has come, I feel;
 I am ready to reveal
Who, or what, has just moved in
 Next door to us.

Lift the flaps and take a look;
 You'll see why I wrote this book . . .

moved in ne

I think we'll leave this miscellanea
And return to Transylvania –
'Cause now we've seen who's just moved in
Next door to us!